Lulu and Lainey

... at the Farm

by: Lois Petren

illustrated by: Tanja Russita

Other books by Lois Petren:

Lulu and Lainey … a French Yarn
Lulu and Lainey … a Christmas Yarn
Lulu and Lainey … the Lucky Day
Lulu and Lainey ... Color with Us

To WDL

ISBN-13: 978-0-0008099-3-8

"Hurry, Lulu, or we'll be late for the train!"

"Yes, Maman!" Lulu called. She picked up her knitting basket and ran to join her parents and brother, Bertie, at the front door.

They were going to her grandparents' farm.

Lulu loved to visit the farm. There were so many interesting things to do such as feeding the animals, playing soccer, and cooking with Grand-mère.

Lulu's favorite animal on the farm was the sheep named Lainey, whose wool her grandmother would spin into her favorite yarn. The yarn was soft and fuzzy.

She even called her favorite ball of yarn "Lainey" because it reminded her of her furry friend.

At the station they got on the train. This was one of Lulu's favorite parts of the trip.

They ate a picnic lunch as they watched the scenery pass by.

Lulu watched as the view changed from city buildings to rolling hills, green fields, and farms.

She was excited ~ this meant they were almost there.

Grand-père was waiting for them at the train station.
Lulu and Bertie ran to him and everyone got a big hug.

They loaded all their luggage into the car and headed to the farm.

Grand-mère was waiting for them at the door of the farm house.

More hugs for everyone!

The next morning Lulu awoke early and Grand-mère was at the door.

She whispered, "Lulu, I have a surprise. Come with me."

They walked to the barn where the animals lived.   There was a newborn baby goat!

Lulu was very happy to see the new kid and couldn't wait until it was old enough to play with her.

There were lots of things to do on the farm.

That morning Lulu helped Grand~mère feed the chickens. They always made her laugh, especially the little chicks.

Lulu helped her grandmother prepare a delicious lunch for the family outside in the garden.

The flowers were blooming and the sun was shining.

After lunch Lulu and Bertie played soccer.

That afternoon Lulu visited Lainey, the sheep.

She looked forward to the next shearing season when there would be more of Lainey's wool to spin. She wondered what color Grand-mère would choose this time. Her favorite was green!

That night while everyone slept the weather became very cold. The wind shook the trees and windows.

The next day Lulu put on a sweater. Everyone stayed inside with a cozy fire and played board games.

Grand-mère returned from the barn
and said, "The weather is too
cold for the baby goat.

We must help!"

She got her knitting basket and chose balls of yarns in different colors. She sat down and began to knit a tiny sweater for the baby goat.

Lulu watched for a while and then went off to play.

After a while Grand-mère called to Lulu: "I don't have enough yarn to finish this sweater. Can I use some of your green yarn?"

Lulu was sad. What if Grand-mère used all of her favorite ball of yarn? She loved it ~ so soft and fuzzy. But the baby goat needed help, so with tears in her eyes, Lulu gave Lainey to her grandmother.

When the sweater was ready Lulu went with her grandmother
to the barn. The baby was huddled close to her mother.

Grand-mère put the little sweater on her.

The baby goat danced around and was so happy to have the sweater to keep her warm.

Lulu could see Lainey's green stripes and was proud to help the baby goat.

Grand-mère asked, "Lulu, what should we name this little kid?" Lulu thought for a moment and said: "Let's call her Lily!"

And so they did.

Lily wore the little sweater until the weather got warm and her own fur was thick enough to protect her.

And Lulu still had enough green yarn left to take home with her!

I hope you enjoyed this book.

Be sure to visit http://www.loisapetren.com to get free coloring pages and learn more about the world of Lulu and Lainey.

CPSIA information can be obtained
at www.ICGtesting.com
Printed in the USA
LVHW071050080419
613324LV00029B/651/P